COUNTING
Aussie Animals
in my backyard

Dedicated to my lil stinkins
Summer, Benny and Jesse

And my support crew
Scotty, Margie and Old Pop

I would like to give special aknowledgement to all of my friends and family that have helped me in the process of creating this book.
All of the childminding, feedback, and encouragement has enabled me to do what I do.
Thank you!
You have helped me achieve something truely beautiful.

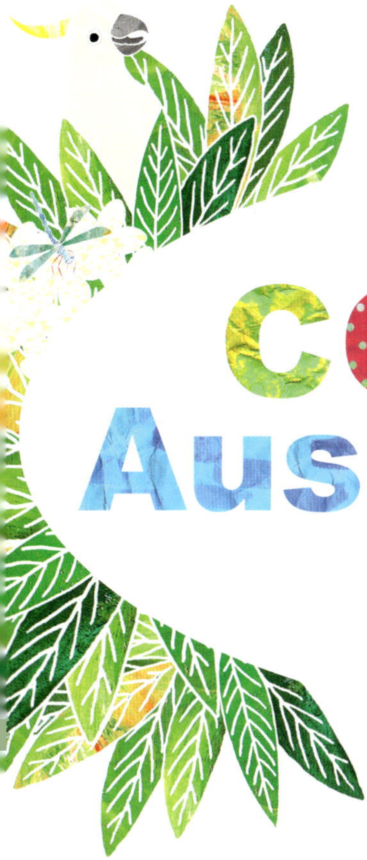

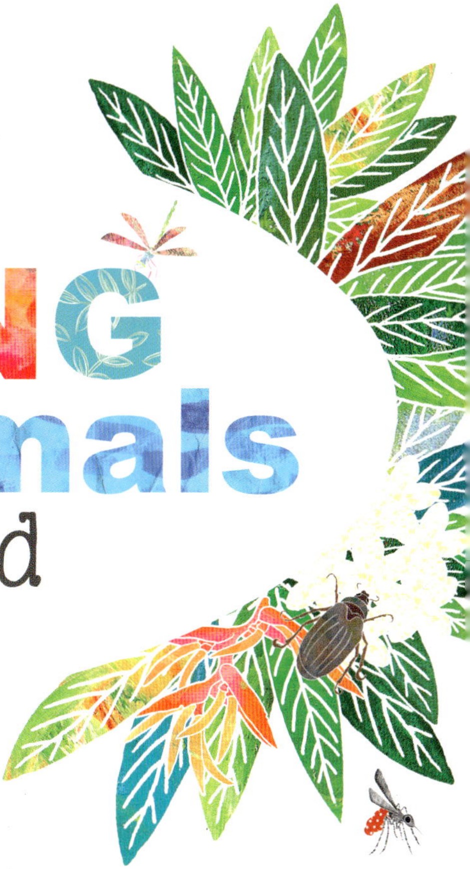

COUNTING Aussie Animals in my backyard

Bronwyn Houston

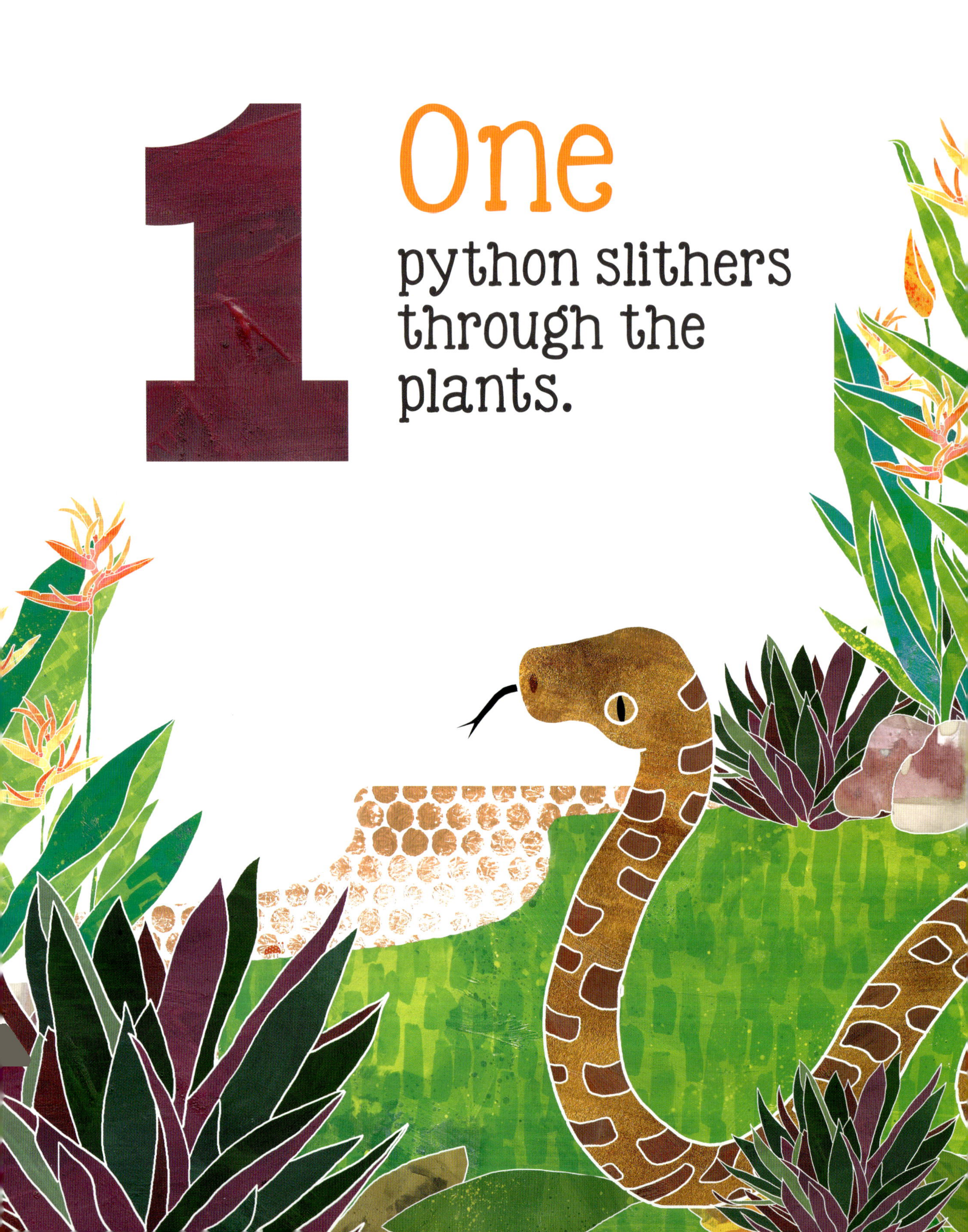

1 One

python slithers through the plants.

2 Two

Two kookaburras laugh on the fence.

3
Three
lizards bask
on a log.

4 Four

frogs hide
in the shade.

5
Five
cockatoos
squawk in
the trees.

6
Six
beetles play
under the
leaves.

7
Seven
dragonflies
dart across
the garden.

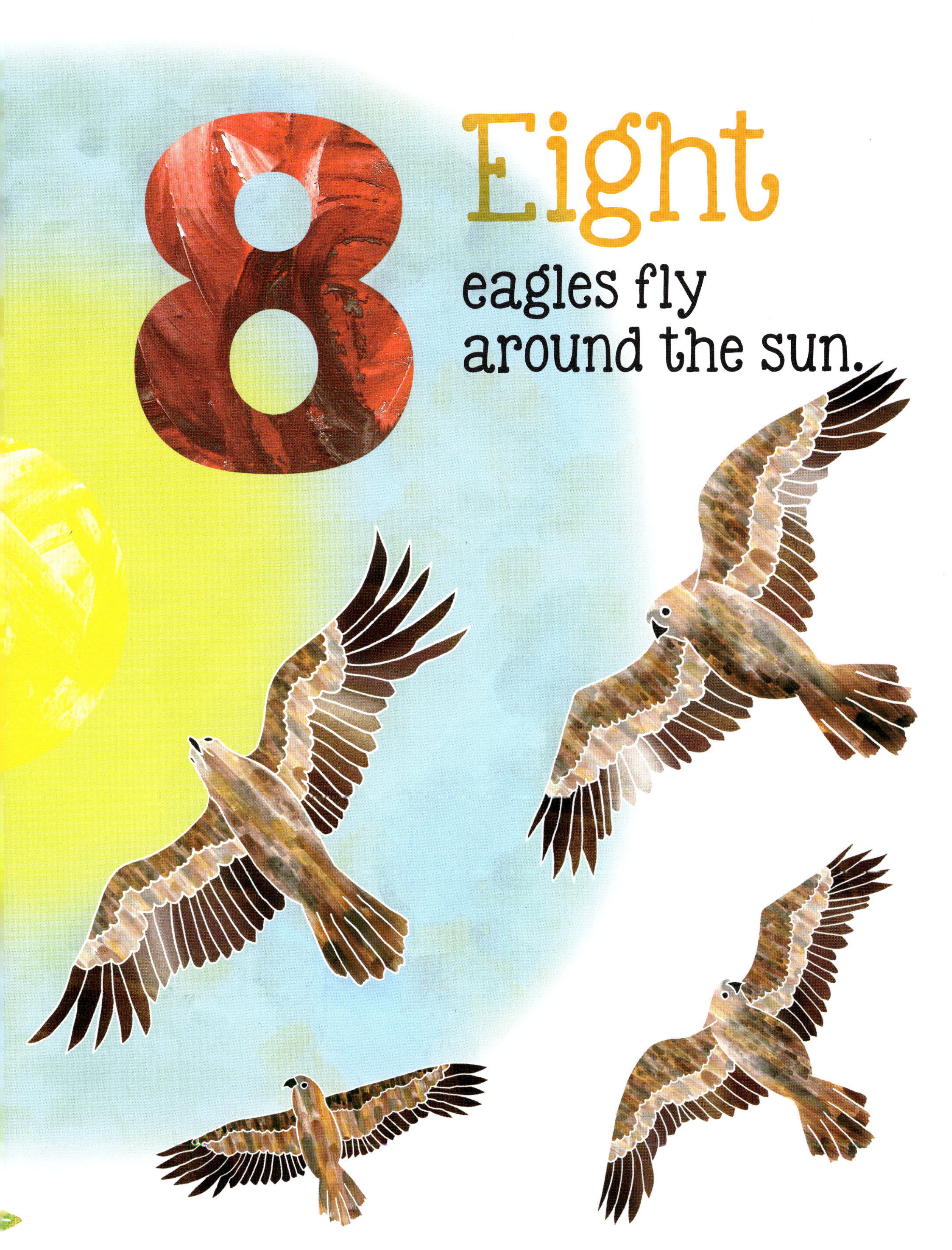

8 Eight

eagles fly
around the sun.

9 Nine

bull ants march
over the hill.

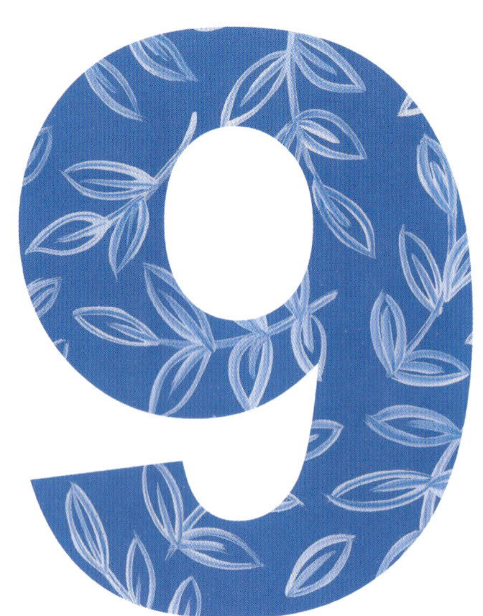

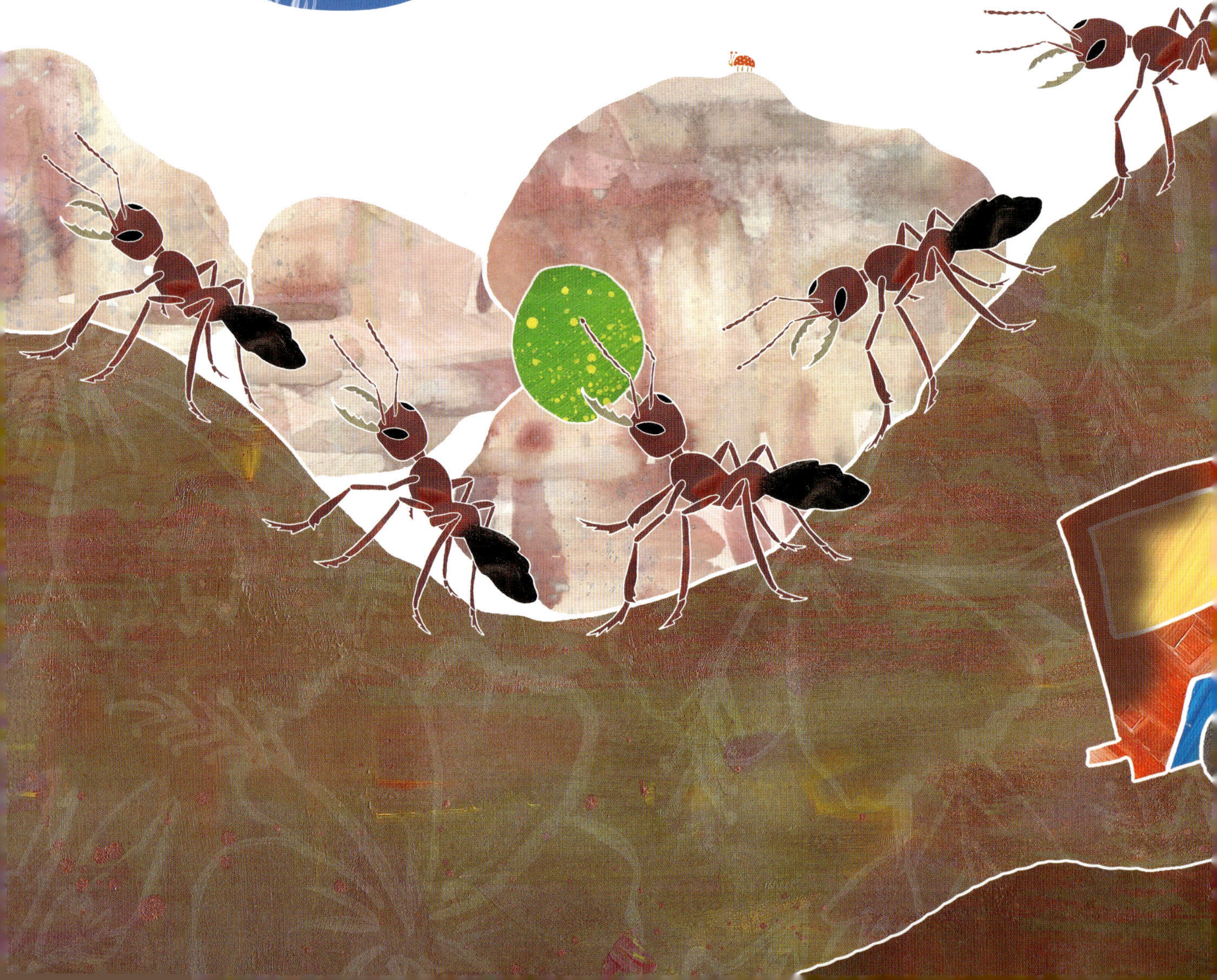

10
Ten
mosquitoes
bite my legs.

First published 2014, reprinted 2014
New paperback edition 2019, reprinted 2019, 2021
Magabala Books Aboriginal Corporation
Broome, Western Australia
Website: www.magabala.com
Email: sales@magabala.com

Magabala Books receives financial assistance from the Commonwealth Government through the Australia Council, its arts advisory body. The State of Western Australia has made an investment in this project through the Department of Local Government, Sport and Cultural Industries. Magabala Books would like to acknowledge the generous support of the Shire of Broome, Western Australia.

Designed by Bronwyn Houston
Reprinted in China by Toppan Leefung Printing Limited

978-1-925768-77-0

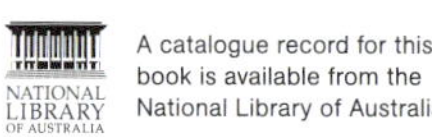

A catalogue record for this book is available from the National Library of Australia

Bronwyn Houston was born in Broome and spent her childhood at the beach, exploring the bush, camping and fishing. Bronwyn finds inspiration from the landscape and colours of Broome, and the natural world around her.

Through her mother's side, She is a proud descendant of the Wunna Nyiyaparli people in the Pilbara region of Western Australia, and her father's family is English and Scottish. She acknowledges with respect the Yawuru people, the Traditional Owners of Broome.

Bronwyn has also published: *Free Diving*, with her Auntie Lorrae Coffin (2017); *Animals in My Garden* (2016); *Return of the Dinosaurs* (2016); *My Home Broome*, with Tamzyne Richardson and friends (2011); *Staircase to the Moon* (2010); and *Loongie the Greedy Crocodile* with Kiefer and Lucy Dan (2008).